Weekly Reader Children's Book Club presents

THE
MANAGING HEN
AND THE
FLOPPY HOUND

Ruth and Latrobe Carroll

pictures by Ruth Carroll

NEW YORK   HENRY Z. WALCK, INC.

Carroll, Ruth
    The managing hen and the floppy hound,
by Ruth and Latrobe Carroll.   Walck,
1972
    unp. illus.

    A story of Floppy, the hound, and
Hester, the hen, on Miss Lucy's farm in
the Great Smoky Mountains.

1. Great Smoky Mountains - Fiction
2. Animals - Stories   3. Farm life -
Fiction   ◯   I. Jt. Auth.
II. Title

Copyright © 1972 by Ruth and Latrobe Carroll
All rights reserved ISBN: 0-8098-1190-1
Library of Congress Catalog Card Number: 70-182532
Printed in the United States of America
Weekly Reader Children's Book Club Edition

For Miriam Babbitt Simpson
and the children of the Barstow School
Kansas City, Missouri

Hester was a little southern hen. She had white feathers, a sharp yellow beak, a crimson comb on top of her head, dark-brown eyes and big yellow feet. She belonged to Miss Lucy Gudger and lived on Miss Lucy's farm in the Great Smoky Mountains.

Hester was a hard-working hen because she liked being busy all the time. But Reuben, the rooster, and the other hens didn't like working much, and the more Hester did, the less they did.

The hardest work was watching over the chicken yard at night. Wild animals would sometimes come tiptoeing very, very softly, hunting for chickens and chicken eggs to eat. It wasn't easy to hear them stealing toward the chicken yard, especially if trees were whispering to each other in a little wind, and the open door of an old shed was squeaking *skreek, skreek,*

skreek on its rusty hinges, and bullfrogs by a pond were twanging, "Let's *glug*, let's *glug*, let's *glug-a-lot*," and a barred owl in thickety woods was booming, "Who are *you*, who are *you*-all?" And it was hard to see things in the black, thick darkness, unless the moon was out.

Hester would doze, first with one eye open and the other eye shut. Then, when the open eye got tired, she would close it and open the shut eye.

When she thought a wildcat or a raccoon or a fox or some other varmint was prowling toward the yard, she'd set up a great squawking and waken all the other chickens. They'd raise such a ruckus, Miss Lucy would run out of her cabin in her nightgown with an old gun

that had belonged to her great-grandfather. She never could see what was frightening the chickens, but she'd fire the gun off, anyhow, pointing it up at the sky. It would make such a *bang* that the varmint, if he was really out there, would forget he was hungry and run away lickety-split.

One day, Miss Lucy brought home a hound-dog pup to help scare off the varmints. He was tan with black spots and deep brown, hopeful eyes. Miss Lucy called him Floppy because his long ears flopped up and down when he ran. And he'd flop when he lay down in a sudden way, ker*flop*.

Floppy's mother was a well-known raccoon hunter,

and his father was famous for hunting foxes. So Miss Lucy hoped he would chase all the varmints away. But the puppy had been too young to learn to hunt raccoons with his mother or foxes with his father. He just liked to chase small hoptoads and try to catch fireflies as they winked and faded against the dark trees.

And Floppy liked Miss Lucy. He followed her round
the farm and watched her milk her cow, Buttercup,
and feed her old mule called Keep-Going and her pig,
Stuffer. He looked and sniffed and listened whenever

she chopped wood, hoed corn and beans and potatoes, and picked or dug up vegetables when they were ready to eat.

But watching and sniffing and listening, as she worked, was not the kind of watching and sniffing and listening Miss Lucy wanted him to do.

"If you don't turn out to be a right-smart watch-dog," she told him, one day—though she knew he couldn't understand a single word—"I reckon I'll have to git me another dog, that's plain as the nose on your face." She put a skinny forefinger on the end of Floppy's nose and he was pleased and licked it. "But I don't know for certain-sure how I could feed *two* dogs—I have hardly enough to feed you, and that's a true fact."

So it was Hester, the hen, who still had to wake everyone up if a varmint came sneaking around. Floppy would wake up last, bark his loudest puppy-barks, which were never very loud, and then go back to sleep.

To Hester, he was just a clumsy nuisance. If he was thirsty, instead of going to the spring nearby, he'd lap up the water in a pan Miss Lucy had set out for the chickens. And when she scattered corn kernels he'd sniff at them. Her scent would still be on them, so he'd scoop some up and move them around in his

mouth, then spit them out because, after all, he didn't like their taste. And he'd get in the way of chickens who wanted insects to eat. He didn't want to eat any insects, he just hoped to get to know them better and maybe play, a little, with them.

Hester tried to keep him out of the chicken yard. Every time she saw him coming she'd ruffle up her feathers, flap her wings and fly at him. "You rabbity, no-account, into-everything pup!" she'd squawk, and do her best to peck him hard. "You're not worth a worm a robin's got a-hold of."

He'd run, zigzagging, away from her. "You ole ganderhead," he'd yip, "what are you so riled up about? I don't mean a mite o' harm, I only want to play. Quit biddy-pecking and jabbing at me." But she would dart at him again and screech, "Food's for eating, not playing. Quit lallygagging round in my yard!"

Floppy tried to remember to keep away from her. He'd go poking and sniffing in the woods, and splashing over rocks in a creek. He'd watch bubbles come floating up from the sandy bottom of the spring and he'd try to catch them and bite them, even though he just kept getting water up his nose.

Hester was glad when Floppy wandered away from the farm, for then she could work at managing all the other hens. She even tried to manage Reuben, the rooster. He liked to strut and crow and mostly laze around. But he didn't enjoy being bossed, and neither did the hens—especially if, when Hester told them they ought to be doing something or other, they were just about to do it all by themselves, anyhow.

Early one morning, before dawn, the woods were hot and still and full of scents. Hester was wide awake. She flapped down from her perch in an old hemlock tree and stood listening to sparrows shrilling thin sounds: quivery, squeezed-out and scared. She couldn't hear any insects; they had crawled deep under piles of leaves, to hide.

She began to cluck and woke up all the other chickens.

"Quit your fussing and fidgeting," grumbled Reuben, the rooster. "Go back to sleep, you hear?"

But Hester wouldn't. "I'm bad worried," she cackled at him, "it's so scary-still. Nary a wildcat nor a raccoon nor a fox nor any such varmint has come a-snooping round the yard. Might be they're afeared o' something and holed up where they feel safe."

"Oh, hush your ole beak!" Reuben squawked. "If you're fixing to have a double duck-fit over nothing, go somewheres else to have it." He tucked his head under a wing, so he couldn't hear her as well, and went right back to sleep.

Floppy wasn't worried, either. He was sound asleep on the porch.

"You addlepated pup!" Hester clucked at him. "You don't know we're in for a heap o' trouble. I calculate a big storm's a-brewing, sure as I got feathers."

But Floppy didn't wake up. And even Miss Lucy, when she came out to scatter corn for the chickens, didn't seem to notice anything strange.

Toward noon, a cool breeze hissed softly through leafy boughs and weeds and grasses. Then came a distant roaring sound. A harsh wind was drawing a blanket across the sky, a thick black cover of rain.

Now all the other chickens were frightened, too. Some flapped up into the hemlock tree. Mother hens with chicks too young to fly up scurried round, looking for shelter under low bushes.

Hester and Reuben were flapping their wings, shooing, pushing, pecking, squawking, trying to make every chick scuttle to safety with its own mother.

Floppy was sitting on the porch. The rising wind and darkness didn't scare him. This was the first storm in his life; he didn't know what a bad storm could do.

All of a sudden, the great wind struck the farm. Big raindrops beat the dry dust in the yard, bouncing up in muddy splashes. The wind swished through the hemlock tree, tossing its branches, rocking its trunk to and fro. Chickens cowering in the tree were holding on tight, crouching low, afraid to lift their heads.

Again and again, lightning split the sky; thunder rolled and crashed.

Hester had done her best to see that all the chickens, big and little, were safe. So now she started to take off for her perch on the hemlock. But a sudden gust picked her up, tearing at her feathers, tossing her this way and that. Upside down, she beat her wings wildly,

squawking, trying to get herself right side up. The rough wind cuffed and pummeled her as it blew her over the yard, then swept her across a clearing, toward the creek. The stream had overflowed its banks and was rushing downward.

For a moment, the wind slackened. Down went Hester, *plop*, into the middle of the creek. The swift waters carried her, squawking and flapping, down, down the mountain.

Miss Lucy was busy inside the cabin. She had closed all the windows and was putting pans and pails under dripping places where the roof leaked. Out on the porch, Floppy had scrouged close to the door.

After an hour or so, the wind began to ease off. Little by little the storm noises stopped, till even the whispering leaves grew still. Now there was just a drip-drip-drip from branches and from the eaves of the cabin's roof.

Up in the sky, torn clouds scudded away; the sun blazed out.

Reuben, the rooster, spread his wings and stretched his neck till it hoisted his head up high. "I'm the biggest rooster in these mountains!" he crowed. "I'll peck the eyes out of any cock who comes sidling up to my hens!"

The hens heard him and clucked to one another, saying, "That *Reuben*, he's a *humdinger!*"

They flapped down out of the hemlock tree or squeezed out, with their chicks, from under bushes. They bustled all about, happy because they had come through the storm alive. "Mighty pretty day for us hens!" they cackled.

It wasn't till Miss Lucy came to feed them, later that afternoon, that they got a surprise. Hester wasn't there to pick out the best corn kernels for herself. At first they were glad she wasn't with them, but then they began to fuss at each other over the choicest tidbits.

Miss Lucy looked all around the yard for Hester. Had something happened to her? "I *do* hope she turns up soon," she said to herself.

Then one of the hens wanted Hester to help her with a chick who just couldn't seem to learn how to dig up a worm for himself and needed scratching lessons.

Another hen wanted Hester's advice about repairing her nest that the storm had damaged.

When some fast-footed squirrels arrived, planning to eat the chickens' corn, Reuben had to do all the scolding and chasing, to keep them out of the yard.

Without any warning, a swift gray shape came skimming over the farm. It was a hungry hawk. But Hester wasn't there to help Reuben get all the chickens

under cover. As he was shooing the last chick under a
bush, the hawk dove straight at him so fast he could
hear the rush of air through wing feathers. Just in

time, he squeezed himself under the bush, then screeched at the hawk pulling out of its dive: "Git away from my flock, you sorry-looking bird! Go home and learn how to fly!"

The hawk made a few more passes over the yard, then flew away. Reuben pushed out from under the bush. He flapped his wings and crowed.

All the rest of the afternoon, the chickens fretted and grumbled. "Where's Hester?" they kept clucking. "Doesn't she *know* she's got work to do here? A frazzling thing, to leave it all to us!"

"Most likely she's traipsing round somewhere," croaked Reuben, "just pleasuring herself." He was hoarse after all his scolding and screeching. His wings ached and his feet hurt. "I declare, I'm plumb tuckered out."

When, at dusk, no Hester came to watch over them, the chickens were downhearted. Reuben didn't even answer when a rooster in the valley crowed, "I'm the fightin'est cock in the mountains, I can lick any rooster around!"

At first, Floppy was glad that Hester wasn't in the chicken yard. He could poke around without her flying at him and trying to peck him. But then the yard didn't seem as exciting, so he moseyed off toward the woods.

When he came to the creek he hardly knew it. Now it was almost a river. He splashed around in shallow places at the edge, looking for trout and crayfish, but they were still hiding from flood waters. So he climbed back onto the bank.

All of a sudden he gave a yip. He had sniffed out a scent—the sharp scent of a fox. He began to run with his nose near the ground, following the long smell that

went on and on. At last he stopped short. There, just ahead of him, he saw a young fox. The fox pup was in a rhododendron thicket, pulling something out of a tangle of branches on the bank of the stream. Floppy saw it was a hen. The fox had her by a wing. She was struggling and squawking feebly.

Floppy moved closer—and then he saw. He knew. It was Hester.

The hair on his back bristled, his tail stiffened and stuck out straight. His lips curled away from his teeth and he snarled, "You let go of that hen, you hear? That's Miss Lucy's hen."

The young fox stopped tugging at Hester's wing. He whirled round to face Floppy. His pointed ears flattened, his tail lashed back and forth. "I don't care whose hen she *was*," he growled. "I caught her. She's *my* hen and I'm fixing to *eat* her."

"You didn't catch her," Floppy barked, "the branches caught her. You're nothing but a pindly pup. You couldn't catch an old lame tortoise if it was crawling uphill."

The fox snapped, "You're nothing but a trifling, rabbity hound-pup. You'd be afeared of a three-legged mouse if it was just one day old!"

"I'm not afeared of *anything*," snarled Floppy. "Start running before I chew you up so your own ma won't know you!"

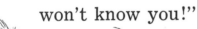

The fox pup began to whine. "You're just not overly smart. Here I up and fetched us a chicken dinner, licking good. We can both eat till our eyes bung out. My stomach's as empty as an eggshell after the chick's got hatched. How about *your* stomach?"

Floppy was often hungry, for Miss Lucy was too poor to feed him much more than table scraps.

"My stomach's mighty hollow," he growled, "so I'm fixing to fill it up with a big juicy fox dinner!"

Floppy had never been in a fight. He had played at fighting with his brothers and sisters, nipping harmless nips, but now he wanted to bite to hurt. He didn't know the best places to bite or the best ways to get his teeth there, but he sprang straight at the fox.

The fox pup jumped to one side and snapped at one of Floppy's long ears, but his jaws missed, he just bit some air. And each time Floppy aimed at a place he felt pretty sure was a good place to bite, that place would suddenly go away, and the fox's teeth would be coming much too close. So Floppy would have to leap out of the way.

The pups whirled and dodged and bumped each other. They fell and they rolled around and jumped up, all the while growling and snarling their fiercest growls and snarls.

At last, the young fox had had enough. With a
wiggle and a twist he jumped clear over Floppy. He
ran away lickety-split.

Floppy began to chase him but stopped short. He had remembered someone. Someone important. *Hester.* She belonged to Miss Lucy. Her place was not in the thicket, it was back in Miss Lucy's chicken yard.

He turned around in a hurry and ran straight back to her. She was still lying in the tangle of branches where the fox had dropped her. Floppy nosed all around her, pushing branches away, poking at her carefully

till he got her free. Gently, very gently, he picked her
up in his mouth. She didn't flap her wings, she didn't
squawk. She hung limp.

Holding his head as high as he could, so she wouldn't
drag on the ground, he carried her up the mountain—
all the way up to Miss Lucy's cabin, then up the steps.
He put her down by the closed door.

Next, he began to bark. He wasn't barking puppy barks now—he was barking loud, big-dog barks. He was trying to tell Miss Lucy, "Look, I've fetched you your hen. Come quick, come *quick!*"

Miss Lucy thought there was a strange dog outside the cabin, making that hullabaloo. She came running out the door, holding up a lantern, to see what was going on.

"Sakes alive!" she cried. "It's *you*, Floppy! You and something else. What *is* it?" She knelt down. "Why, it's *Hester!*" She picked the hen up and looked her all over, touching her here and there. Hester lay still. Both her eyes were closed. In a moment, though, she opened one eye and blinked.

"Why, I declare," Miss Lucy said, "you're the wettest, sorriest, messiest hen I ever laid eyes on. But I reckon you're not hurt, any—just tuckered out."

She got an old towel and dried Hester off as best she could. Then she covered her with another towel and put her down on the floor of the porch. "Most likely you'll perten up mighty soon," she said.

Then she patted Floppy's back and stroked his neck

and rubbed him behind his ears. "Smart dog," she said, "mighty smart, to find my poor ole hen and tote her here to me so gentle. Smart dog, *smart dog!*"

That was the first time Miss Lucy had ever made a fuss over Floppy. His tail went from side to side, then it swished round and round in circles. It wagged so hard, it wiggled the rest of him.

Miss Lucy went to bed. Floppy lay down on the porch, to rest. Hester tried to get up but she couldn't,

then she tried again and again till she could. She wobbled over to Floppy and pecked him on a toe. But this time her pecking was different; it was just a gentle, friendly poke, Clucking, she settled down on his stomach, which began to warm and dry her damp feathers. He felt her resting snug against him. She would soon be back, managing the chicken yard, he hoped.

Before long, she dozed off. But Floppy stayed awake, wide awake. He wanted to keep watch. He was tired of puppy play: chasing hoptoads, fireflies and such. He wanted to play big-dog games. Now that he was older, his ears were better at telling what sound was what. His nose knew which smell was which. His teeth were bigger, his legs were much stronger, and so were his barks and his growls.

He felt all ready, through and through, to guard Miss Lucy's farm, for no one but Miss Lucy herself knew it as well as he did. He knew what Hester and Reuben and her other chickens did, and what her pig, Stuffer, did, and what her cow, Buttercup, did, and what her old mule, Keep-Going, did, and what Miss Lucy herself did, and he wanted them all to keep doing all those things. So he was ready to run off the farm any fox or wildcat or raccoon or any other varmint who might plan to pester any of them or eat any up.

He licked his nose so it could smell varmints better. He sniffed and felt proud.